THE OLD-FASHIONED CHILDREN'S STORYBOOK

WANDERER BOOKS

Published by Simon & Schuster, New York

Published by WANDERER BOOKS
A Simon & Schuster Division of
Gulf & Western Corporation
Simon & Schuster Building
1230 Avenue of the Americas
New York, New York 10020

Published under arrangement with
Ottenheimer Publishers, Inc.

Thanks are due to Heinemann Limited &
J. B. Lippincott Company for permission to reproduce
illustrations by Arthur Rackham from Rip Van Winkle,
by Washington Irving, reissued 1967.

Manufactured in the United States of America
10 9 8 7 6 5 4 3 2 1

WANDERER and colophon are trademarks
of Simon & Schuster

Library of Congress Cataloging in Publication Data
Main entry under title:

The Old-fashioned children's storybook.

SUMMARY: A collection of well-known fairy tales,
fables, stories, poems, and nursery rhymes, illustrated
by some of the greatest children's illustrators of all
time.
   1. Children's literature. [1. Literature—
Collections]   I. Flax, Zena.
PZ5.045   808.8'99282   80-16258
ISBN 0-671-41540-9 (Simon & schuster)

FOREWORD
by Naomi Lewis

Within these pages lies a rare combination of the most cherished children's stories and rhymes, beautifully accented by the finest of children's illustrators. This delicate blending is something not easily found today. This volume offers a taste of the work of six of these artists, and of what might have been found in the luckier homes a century ago.

The elegant, internationally-esteemed Walter Crane (1845-1915) illustrates several of the greatest fairy tales, with rich, meticulous detail, a clear use of color, and deep emotion.

Randolph Caldecott (1846-1886), the most cheerfully vigorous of all the artists here, achieved much in the short time he was alive. His unique style was gentle and spirited as well as tough and rustic, making his country scenes come alive.

Kate Greenaway (1846-1901) invented a manner which has kept her name alive for a hundred years and her works steadily reprinted today. She was a superb designer,

able to catch in her simple country scenes something of her own childhood love of meadows, gardens, and flowers. Disliking the stiff, hot, starchy clothes imposed on Victorian children, she conceived freer dress in her illustrations—subsequently influencing children's fashions.

The work of Louis Maurice Boutet de Monvel (1850-1913), one of the earliest and most distinguished of the new-color illustrators for children in France, captures in soft and simple, muted colors the charm and amusements of the countryside.

The engaging, dreamlike pictures for the two Robert Louis Stevenson poems reflect the genius of American artist Jessie Willcox Smith (1863-1935). Her gifts came to light in an odd way: as a young girl studying to become a kindergarten teacher, she was asked to "chaperone" a drawing class at a boy's school. To occupy herself, she also drew, and developed her own presentation of scenes full of flowers, fairies, and children.

Arthur Rackham (1876-1930), London-born, drew from childhood (on pillows if paper was forbidden), studied at the Slade School and in Paris, and had his first of many triumphs with Grimm's fairy tales (1900). A typical Rackham scene is one with gnarled and gnomelike trees, autumn mood, dim light, strong and eerie lines, and the prevailing mushroom greys and browns.

It is not difficult to see why the children of centuries past craved pictures as well as rhymes and stories. Not only was there no television, but also no photography, or colour reproductions. Most great paintings were owned privately, not displayed in museums. Castles, cities, mountains, the sea itself were often matters of dream. Through pictures the unknown became visible — and the visible offered glimpses of the unknown.

For, make no mistake; if you were flown into a country village a century back, you could not count on meeting a Greenaway child, a Rackham gnome, a forest of silver, a talking hind. The great age of the illustrated fairy tale was also the age of railways, mills, and furnaces. Yet in the country of the mind these things are real enough. The green May morning of Greenaway keeps its freshness; summer stays always summer in Stevenson's garden; on the Catskill Mountains one can still hear strange cries for help; the Rackham thunder and twilight never lose their power to thrill. And this land has a personal key for those wishing to enter—you have only to open a book such as this, to look at the pictures, and read.

CONTENTS

BEAUTY
AND THE BEAST

Illustrated by Walter Crane

Once upon a time a rich Merchant lost all his money and had to live in a small cottage with his three daughters. The two elder girls grumbled at this; but the youngest, called Beauty, tried to comfort her father and make his new home happy.

One day the Merchant was going on a journey, and his daughters came to wish him goodbye; the two elder told him to bring them some fine presents on his return, but Beauty only asked him to bring her a rose.

When the Merchant was on his way home, he saw some lovely roses and, thinking of Beauty, picked the prettiest he could find. He had no sooner taken it than a hideous Beast appeared and threatened to kill him for stealing the rose. The Merchant stammered that he had taken the rose only to please his daughter Beauty. Hearing this, the Beast said gruffly, "Well, I will spare your life, if one of your daughters will come here, willingly, to die instead of you."

Sadly the Merchant returned home with the rose and his daughters ran out to greet him. Giving Beauty the rose, he told her everything. Beauty said that, as her rose was the cause of all this trouble, she alone must suffer for it.

When she reached the Beast's palace, the Beast asked her: "Beauty, did you come here willingly to die in place of your father?" Willingly," she answered with a trembling voice.

For her bravery the Beast said she should not die, but live in his palace instead. He gave her a fine room and all her meals were served to the sound of music. At supper time the Beast would sit and talk with her so pleasantly that she soon became less afraid of him. One day he asked her, "Am I so very ugly?" "I am afraid you are," replied Beauty,

"but then you are so kind that I don't mind your looks." "Would you marry me then?" he said. Beauty, looking away, said, "Pray don't ask me." So the Beast went sadly away.

Beauty was now, in fact, quite the Queen of the palace, but she was always alone except at supper-time, when the Beast appeared and talked so pleasantly that she liked him more and more. But each time he asked her, "Beauty, will you marry me?", she always shook her head, and he would slip quietly and sadly away.

Although Beauty had everything she could wish for, she could not forget her father and sisters. At last, one day she begged so hard to

go home that the Beast agreed. He gave her a ring, telling her to place it on her dressing-table whenever she wanted to leave his palace or return to it.

That night she placed the ring on her dressing-table and the next morning she was overjoyed to wake up in her father's house. She flung her arms round her father's neck and gave him presents from the Beast.

When she had stayed some weeks with her family, Beauty remembered her promise to the Beast, and decided to return to him. But her father begged her to stay a day or two longer, so she agreed. Then one night she dreamed that the poor Beast was lying dead in his palace garden; she awoke in a fright, looked for her ring, and placed it on the dressing-table. In the morning she awoke at the palace and ran to the place in the garden that she had dreamed about. There, sure enough, was the poor Beast lying senseless on his back.

Beauty wept bitterly, reproaching herself for causing his death. She ran to a fountain and sprinkled his face with water. The Beast opened his eyes and, as soon as he could speak, he said sorrowfully, "Now that I see you once more, I die contented!" "No, no!" she cried, "you shall not die! Oh, live to be my husband, and Beauty will be your faithful wife!" The moment she had uttered these words, a dazzling light shone everywhere, the palace windows glittered with lamps, and music was heard all around. To her great wonder, a handsome young Prince stood before her. He told her her words had broken the spell of a magician, by which he had been doomed to remain in the shape of the Beast, until a beautiful girl should love him in spite of his ugliness.

The grateful Prince now claimed Beauty as his wife, to the delight of her father, the Merchant.

Illustrated by Kate Greenaway

Pɪᴘᴇ thee high, and pipe thee low,
Let the little feet go faster;
Blow your penny trumpet–blow!
Well done, little master!

Lɪᴛᴛʟᴇ Miss Patty
and Master Paul
Have found two snails
on the garden wall.
"These snails," said Paul,
"how slow they walk!
A great deal slower
than we can talk.
Make haste, Mr. Snail,
travel quicker, I pray;
In a race with our tongues
you'd be beaten to-day."

THE MILKMAID
Illustrated by
M. Boutet de Monvel

One day a milkmaid was on her way to market to sell a pitcher of milk. As she walked, she thought about the money she would get for the milk. "I shall buy four chickens with the money," she said to herself. "And the chickens will lay a hundred eggs. And the eggs will hatch more chickens. And when I sell those chickens I will have enough money to buy a pig!"

"The pig will grow bigger and bigger every day. Soon I will sell the pig for even more money."

"I will then buy a cow and a sweet little baby calf!" said the milkmaid. She was so happy that she started to skip. You can guess what happened! She dropped the pail and the milk spilled all over the road.

The milkmaid cried all the way home and, when she got home, her father said "Daughter, you must never count chickens before they are hatched."

RIP VAN WINKLE

Illustrated by Arthur Rackham

Long, long ago, in a far-off land, a small village lay at the foot of tall, wooded mountains. The village was a pleasant one, with neat, well-built houses. In one of these houses (which, sad to say, was not as tidy as the others) lived Rip Van Winkle and his family.

Rip was a simple, good-natured fellow, popular with his neighbours, and a special favourite of the village children, who loved to play with him or listen to his exciting stories of witches and ghosts.

But Rip had one great fault. He did not like work. Not that he ever refused to help a neighbour, but as to keeping his own farm in order – this he declared was impossible. The animals went astray, his crops failed, his fields were full of weeds. His children, too, ran wild and his son seemed to have inherited the worst faults of his father.

If left to himself, Rip would have whistled his life away in perfect contentment, but his wife continually kept shouting about his idleness. Day after day she would nag about the ruin he was bringing on his family until, when he could listen no longer, he would go down to the village inn with his dog, Wolf. There, with his friends, he spent many happy hours in gossip. Sometimes, when the nagging got very bad Rip would take his gun to go shooting in the mountains, accompanied by Wolf.

His children ran ragged and wild

They climbed a narrow gully

On this particular day, Rip had climbed higher than usual, and just as he was about to return home he heard a voice call "Rip Van Winkle!" He looked round but, seeing nothing, he turned to climb down the mountain. As he did so, he heard the same cry: "Rip Van Winkle! Rip Van Winkle!"

Wolf growled and, creeping close to his master's side, looked fearfully towards the valley below.

Looking now anxiously in the same direction, Rip saw a strange, weird figure beckoning for help. As he approached, Rip saw that the stranger was a short, old man, with a thick, bushy beard, and that he was wearing quaint, old-fashioned clothes. On his shoulder was a barrel, seemingly full of drink. Sharing the weight of the barrel, the two men clambered in silence up a narrow cleft in the mountain.

As they climbed, Rip could hear noises like distant thunder but, thinking it only a far-off thunderstorm, followed the stranger up the mountain until he came to an open patch of ground.

He even dared to taste the drink

As he drew near, his eyes opened wide with astonishment, for in the clearing were very odd-looking men drinking and playing skittles. They were all elderly, with long beards and dressed in an old-fashioned style. What seemed particularly odd was that, though these old folk were

He fell into a deep sleep

obviously enjoying themselves, their faces were sad and they played in silence. All that could be heard was the noise of the rolling skittle balls, which echoed in the mountains like the rumbling of thunder.

Rip's silent companion poured the contents of the barrel into large beakers, and then indicated that Rip should pass them round. Gradually, Rip's fears lessened and, curious to discover what the others were enjoying, he tasted the drink while no one was looking. Realising how thirsty he was, he drank more and more until, feeling drowsy, he lay down on a patch of grass and fell into a deep sleep.

On waking, Rip found himself at the place where he had first met the stranger. He rubbed his eyes. "Surely," he thought, "I haven't slept here all night." He looked around for his gun, but all he could see was a rusty firelock. He whistled for Wolf—but in vain. No dog was to be seen. As he got up, his joints felt stiff. Utterly bewildered, he picked up the rusty gun and, with difficulty, made his way home.

As he drew near the village, a band of children ran after him and mocked

*The dogs barked
at him as he passed*

him. Looking down at his clothes, he saw just how ragged and old they were.

When he entered the village Rip met a number of people—but none of whom he recognised. He entered his house—but it was empty. He called for his wife and children—but there was only silence. He went to the village inn—but that, too, was gone. In its place was a large, ricketty building, in front of which stood a crowd of people arguing angrily.

Suddenly, someone turned round to ask Rip his opinion. He did not know how to answer. He merely said he was looking for his companions who used to gather at the inn, and mentioned some names. An old man turned round in surprise. "Why!" he declared, "they've all been dead for twelve years or more."

Rip was saddened by this news, and also puzzled by the enormous lapse of time. Out of despair he cried, "Does anybody here know Rip Van Winkle?" "Oh, yes", answered one or two people, "there he is, leaning against the tree." Rip looked up, and there saw himself as a young man.

By now Rip was at his wits' end. "Last night," he exclaimed, "I went to sleep. I woke up to discover my gun had been changed, and my dog had disappeared. Now somebody else is me!"

People began winking and nodding at each other as if to say "Poor old man —he's mad" and, as they did so, a young woman passed by, holding a crying baby. "Hush, Rip," she said, "the old man won't hurt you." The name of the child and the sound of the woman's voice sparked off something in Rip's mind. "What is your name?" he asked. "Judith Gardenier," she replied. "And your father's name?" "Ah, Rip Van Winkle was his name. It is twenty years since he left home with his

The most ancient inhabitant of the village

gun and dog—and he has never been heard of since." Rip could contain himself no longer. Filled with emotion, he cried, "I am your father—young once, now old. Does no one recognise poor Rip Van Winkle?"

The crowd stood amazed. Rip told his story and it was decided to ask the opinion of the village's most ancient inhabitant, who remembered Rip at once. He told how for many, many years it was said that the mountains were haunted; that his own father had seen strange men playing skittles, and had heard the noise of their skittle balls rolling like distant thunder.

Rip was happily re-united with his daughter and went to live with her family — although his son was still as idle.

Rip would tell his peculiar tale to every stranger who came to the village. Some people re-fused to believe it. But the village inhabitants were all quite sure it was true and, to this very day, whenever they run in from a thunderstorm on a summer's afternoon, they say that the old men are having a game of skittles.

They run indoors
from summer
thunderstorms

P OOR Dicky's dead!—The bell we toll,
   And lay him in the deep, dark hole.
The sun may shine, the clouds may rain,
But Dick will never pipe again!
His quilt will be as sweet as ours—
Bright buttercups and cuckoo flowers.

Illustrated by Kate Greenaway

THE FROG
AND
THE OX

**Illustrated by
M. Boutet de Monvel**

Mr. Frog and his son were hopping along a field. They stopped next to a big ox. "Look, Father," said the little frog, "isn't he the biggest thing you ever saw?"

"He's not so big," Mr. Frog said, "I can be as big as he is. Look!" and he took a deep breath and expanded his chest.

"The ox is still bigger," the little frog said to his father. And so Mr. Frog took a deeper breath and expanded his chest still more.

"You are getting bigger, father. But still the ox is greater in size than you are."
And Mr. Frog took still a bigger breath and expanded his chest even further.

Then POP! Poor Mr. Frog burst like a balloon!
We must not try to be what others are. It is best
to be yourself.

THE HIND IN THE WOOD

Illustrated by Walter Crane

Once upon a time there lived a King and Queen who were very happy together but sad that they had no child.

At long last, a Princess was born, whom they named Desiree. At her christening her Fairy Godmother gave her the gifts of beauty, wit, good health, and so on, but warned of a witch's curse that if she should see the light of day before she became sixteen, it would perhaps cost her her life.

Horrified, the King and Queen decided to build a palace without doors or windows until the Princess should be sixteen . . .

The Princess grew up beautiful and clever and the Queen sent a portrait of her to the greatest courts. of the world. A Prince,

Andrew, loved it so much that he begged his father, the King, to send an Ambassador to ask for the hand of the Princess in marriage. Her parents were delighted and agreed, and Desiree would spend all day looking at a portrait of the Prince.

However, there were still three months to go before she should be sixteen. The Ambassador told her parents that Prince Andrew would die of love if he did not see the Princess immediately. The Queen was worried about the witch's curse, but the Princess suggested that she travelled in a coach so closely shut that she could not see daylight.

The King and Queen thought this was a very good idea. A coach

was built without windows, lined with pink and silver brocade and Desiree was locked in it with her lady in waiting, Jacqueline. Jacqueline did not like the Princess and was in love with Prince Andrew whose portrait she had seen. So, about midday on the first day when the sun was shining very brightly, the jealous Jacqueline suddenly slashed through the coach lining with a large knife. Light flooded in, and the Princess turned into a white hind and ran off to hide herself in the shade of the forest trees.

Jacqueline, who was as ugly as the Princess was beautiful, dressed herself in Desiree's best clothes and reached the city to be met by Prince Andrew and his father. However, they were not deceived, and had the false Princess arrested and shut up in their castle dungeon.

Prince Andrew was so upset at the loss of Desiree that he decided to leave the court secretly and find some lonely place in which to spend the rest of his sad life. At the end of three days he found himself in a vast forest — the very one in which Desiree was roaming as a hind.

Her Fairy Godmother had heard of Desiree's misfortune, and suddenly appeared to her as she was wandering miserably about the wood. Desiree begged to be restored to her natural form. "I cannot do that," said the fairy, "but I can help you a little. As soon as night falls, you will become yourself again but, as soon as it is dawn, you must turn back into a hind. For the time being follow this path and you will come to a little cottage where an old woman lives. Tell her everything and she will give you shelter." So saying, the fairy disappeared.

Desiree followed her directions and found the cottage and a little woman seated by the door. Hearing Desiree's story, the old woman gave her a very pretty room to rest in. As soon as it was quite dark, Desiree turned—much to her delight—back from a hind into a Princess.

Meanwhile, the Prince, still wandering in the wood, reached the cottage and asked the old woman for food and shelter for the night.

The next day as he was walking in the forest, he saw a hind running past and shot an arrow at it. This hind was none other than Desiree, but her Fairy Godmother preserved her from being hit. The Prince lost sight of her and, being very tired, gave up the chase. He lay down and went to sleep. The hind crept back to the same spot and, recognising him from his portrait, touched him gently. This awoke the Prince and he jumped up startled. The Hind darted off into the woods and he shot an arrow at her, hitting her foreleg. She fell down, and the Prince, greatly grieved to see her bleeding, gathered some herbs, bound them round her leg and made her a bed of branches.

Just then the old woman passed by. "Look at the hind I have caught," claimed the Prince. "My lord," replied the old woman," this hind belonged to me before she did to you. I would much sooner lose my life than her," and so the Prince generously gave her up.

That evening, hearing sounds in the next room, the Prince made a hole in the wall large enough to see through. Amazed, he saw the Princess in her beautiful dress and the old woman bandaging her arm. "Alas!" said the Princess, "must I become a hind every day and see the Prince, the man I love, without being able to speak to him?" Recognising the Princess from her portrait, the Prince immediately knocked gently on the door and ran to Desiree.

"What," he exclaimed, "were you the white hind I injured with my arrow?" Desiree assured him that she was all right and spoke to him so kindly that he could not doubt her love for him. They decided they would return to her castle immediately to be married.

All this was brought about by the Fairy Godmother. The pretty cottage in the wood was hers, and she herself was the old woman.

Illustrated by Kate Greenaway

O RING the bells! O ring the bells!
We bid you, sirs, good morning; Give thanks, we pray, our flowers are gay,
And fair for your adorning.

O ring the bells! O ring the bells!
Good sirs, accept our greetings;
Where we have been, the woods are green.
So, hey! for our next meeting.

THE FLOWERS

Illustrated by
Jessie Willcox Smith

ALL the names I know from nurse:
Gardener's garters, Shepherd's purse,
Bachelor's buttons, Lady's smock,
And the Lady Hollyhock.

Fairy places, fairy things,
Fairy woods where the wild bee wings,
Tiny trees for tiny dames
These must all be fairy names!

Tiny woods below whose boughs
Shady fairies weave a house;
Tiny tree-tops, rose or thyme,
Where the braver fairies climb!

Fair are grown-up people's trees,
But the fairest woods are these;
Where, if I were not so tall,
I should live for good and all.

You SEE merry Phillis, that dear little maid,
Has invited Belinda to tea;
Her nice little garden is shaded by trees
What pleasanter place could there be?

There's a cake full of plums,
there are strawberries too,
And the table is set on the green;
I'm fond of a carpet all daisies and grass,
Could a prettier picture be seen?

Illustrated by Kate Greenaway

SCHOOL is over,
Oh, what fun!
Lessons finished,
Play begun.
Who'll run fastest,
You or I?
Who'll laugh loudest?
Let us try.

THE HARE AND THE TORTOISE

Illustrated by M. Boutet de Monvel

"I will race you to that tree," said the Tortoise to the Hare, "and I'll bet that I will win!"

The Hare laughed and laughed. Why, he could win with one hop!"

"Go on then", he said, "I'll let you start first."

The Tortoise plodded along slowly. The Hare ate some grass and in a little while fell asleep.

When he awoke, the Tortoise was just getting to the tree. The Hare hopped quickly and, in two hops, he was at the tree. But it was too late. The Tortoise had won! "Slow and steady wins the race!"

THE
FROG PRINCE

Illustrated by Walter Crane

Once upon a time the youngest daughter of a King was playing by a fountain, tossing a golden ball into the air, and it fell into a fountain.

She began to sob, and a voice croaked, "Why are you crying?" She saw a Frog stretching his thick ugly head out of the water.

"Do not cry," said the Frog, "What will you give me if I fetch your golden ball up again?" "Anything, dear Frog," said she, "My dresses, my jewels, or my coronet." The Frog answered, "If you will promise to love me, and let me be your companion, sit at your table, eat from your golden plate, drink from your cup, and sleep in your little bed, I will dive down and fetch your golden ball."

"Oh, you can have all these," said she, "if you will only get it for me"–not meaning to keep her promise. The Frog dived down and got the ball for her

and, delighted, she ran off immediately. "Stop! stop!" cried the Frog.

The next day, when the King's daughter was sitting at table, she heard something coming up the marble stairs, *splish-splash, splish-splash*. There was knock at the door, and a voice said, "Open the door to me, youngest daughter of the King!"

She opened the door and, when she caught sight of the Frog, she shut

it again hurriedly and sat down at the table, looking very pale. The King asked her jokingly whether a giant had come to fetch her away.

"Oh, no!" answered she; "it is no giant, but an ugly Frog," and she told her father of her promise. "I must tell you I promised him he should be my companion, but I never thought that he could come out of the water."

Then the King said, "You must always do what you have promised – go and let him in." So the King's daughter opened the door, and the Frog hopped in right up to her chair, jumped on the table and ate from her own golden plate. The Frog seemed to enjoy his dinner very much, but every bit that the Princess ate nearly choked her.

At last the Frog said "I feel very tired; please carry me upstairs now into your bedroom, so that I may rest." At this, the Princess began to cry, for she was afraid of the slimy cold Frog, and dared not touch him; and besides, he actually wanted to sleep in her own beautiful, clean bed.

But her tears only made the King very angry, and he said, "He helped you when you needed help—now you must keep your promise to him!" So she took the Frog up gingerly with two fingers, and put him in a corner of her bedroom. But as she got into bed, he hopped up to it, and said, "I will sleep better in bed than on the floor." This speech put the Princess in a terrible rage and, picking the Frog up, she threw him with all her strength against the wall,

saying, "Now, will you be quiet, you ugly Frog?"

But, as he fell, he was changed from a Frog into a handsome Prince. Then he told her how an evil witch had turned him into a Frog, and that no one but herself had the power to take him out of the fountain. The next day, with her father's consent, they were married and went to live in his own kingdom.

Illustrated by Kate Greenaway

WHICH is the way to Somewhere Town?
Oh, up in the morning early;
Over the tiles and the chimney-pots,
That is the way, quite clearly.

BOWL away! bowl away!
Fast as you can;
He who can fastest bowl,
He is my man!

Up and down, round about,
Don't let it fall;
Ten times, or twenty times,
Beat, beat them all!

Up you go, shuttlecocks, ever so high!
Why come you down again, shuttlecocks—why?
When you have got so far, why do you fall?
Where all are high, which is highest of all?

THE BOAT sails away, like a bird on the wing,
And the little boys dance on the sands in a ring.

The wind may fall, or the wind may rise—
You are foolish to go; you will stay if you're wise.

The little boys dance, and the little girls run:
If it's bad to have money, it's worse to have none.

JESSIE WILLCOX SMITH.

MY SHADOW

Illustrated by
Jessie Willcox Smith

I HAVE A LITTLE shadow that goes in and out with me,
And what can be the use of him is more than I can see.
He is very, very like me from the heels up to the head;
And I see him jump before me, when I jump into my bed.

THE FUNNIEST thing about him is the way he likes to grow
Not at all like proper children, which is always very slow;
For he sometimes shoots up taller like an india-rubber ball,
And he sometimes gets so little that there's none of him at all.

HE HASN'T got a notion of how children ought to play,
And can only make a fool of me in every sort of way.
He stays so close beside me, he's a coward you can see;
I'd think shame to stick to nursie as that shadow sticks to me!

ONE MORNING, very early, before the sun was up,
I rose and found the shining dew on every buttercup;
But my lazy little shadow, like an arrant sleepy-head,
Had stayed at home behind me and was fast asleep in bed.

Illustrated by Kate Greenaway

THE finest, biggest fish, you see,
Will be the trout that's caught by me,
But if the monster will not bite,
Why, then I'll hook a little mite.

1, 2. One Two,
Buckle my shoe.

3, 4. Three, Four,
Open the door.

Illustrated by Walter Crane

ELIZABETH, Elsbeth,
Betsy, and Bess,
They all went together
to seek a bird's nest
They found a bird's nest
with five eggs in;
They all took one,
and left four in.

5, 6. Five, Six, Pick up sticks. 7, 8. Seven, Eight, Lay them straight.

JACK Sprat would eat no fat,
His wife would eat no lean;
But between the two of them
They licked the platter clean.

9, 10.
Nine, Ten,
A good fat Hen.

NEEDLES and pins,
needles and pins,
When a man marries
his trouble begins.

52

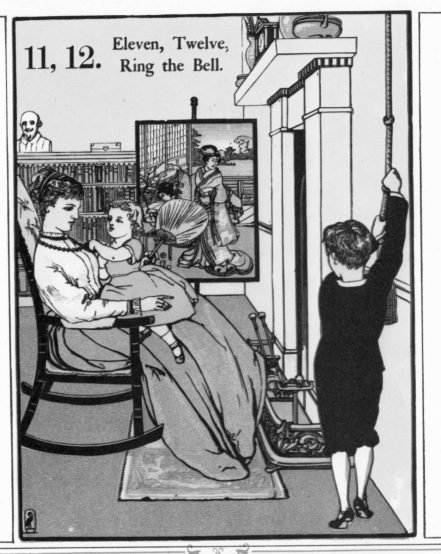

11, 12. Eleven, Twelve,
Ring the Bell.

MISTRESS Mary,
 Quite contrary,
How does your garden grow?
 With silver bells,
 And cockle shells,
And cowslips all in a row.

13, 14. Thirteen, Fourteen, Maids are courting.

RIDE A-cock horse to Banbury Cross,
To see an old woman get up
on her horse;
Rings on her fingers
and bells at her toes,
And so she makes music
wherever she goes.

15, 16. Fifteen, Sixteen, Maids in the Kitchen.

S IMPLE Simon met a pieman,
Going to the fair;
Says Simple Simon
to the pieman,
"Let me taste your ware!"

17, 18. Seventeen, Eighteen,
Maids in waiting.

CROSS **X** patch,
  Draw the latch,
Sit by the fire and spin:
    Take a cup
    And drink it up,
Then call the neighbours in.

19, 20. Nineteen, Twenty.
My plate is empty.

YOU know Monday
is Sunday's brother;
Tuesday is such another;
Wednesday go to church and pray;
Thursday is half-holiday;
On Friday it's too late to spin,
And Saturday is half-holiday again.

HEY DIDDLE, DIDDLE

Illustrated by Randolph Caldecott

Hey, diddle, diddle,
The cat and the fiddle,

The cow jumped over
the moon.

The little dog laughed
to see such fun,

And the dish ran away with the spoon.

THE HOUSE THAT JACK BUILT

Illustrated by Randolph Caldecott

THIS is the **House** that Jack built.

This is the **Malt,**
That lay in the House
that Jack built.

This is the **Rat,**
That ate the Malt,
That lay
in the House
that Jack built.

This is the **Cat,**
That killed the Rat,
That ate the Malt,
That lay in the House
that Jack built.

This is the **Dog**
That worried the Cat,
That killed the Rat,
That ate the Malt
That lay in the House
that Jack built.

This is the **Cow**
with the
crumpled horn,
That tossed
the Dog,
That worried
the Cat,
That killed the Rat,
That ate the Malt,
That lay
in the House
that Jack built

This is the **Maiden** all forlorn,
That milked the Cow with the crumpled horn
That tossed the Dog,
That worried the Cat,
That killed the Rat,
That ate the Malt,
That lay in the House that Jack built.

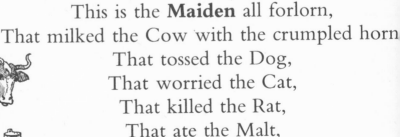

This is the **Man** all tattered and torn,
That kissed the Maiden all forlorn,
That milked the Cow with the crumpled horn,
That tossed the Dog,
That worried the Cat,
That killed the Rat,
That ate the Malt,
That lay in the House that Jack built.

This is the **Priest,** all shaven and shorn,
That married the Man all tattered and torn,
That kissed the Maiden all forlorn,
That milked the Cow with the crumpled horn,
That tossed the Dog,
That worried the Cat,
That killed the Rat,
That ate the Malt,
That lay in the House that Jack built.

This is the **Cock** that crowed in the morn,
That waked the Priest all shaven and shorn,
That married the Man all tattered and torn,
That kissed the Maiden all forlorn,
That milked the Cow with the crumpled horn,
That tossed the Dog,
That worried the Cat,
That killed the Rat,
That ate the Malt,
That lay in the House—that Jack built.

This is the **Farmer** who sowed the corn,
That fed the Cock that crowed in the morn,
That waked the Priest all shaven and shorn,
That married the Man all tattered and torn,
That kissed the Maiden all forlorn,
That milked the Cow with the crumpled horn,
That tossed the Dog,
That worried the Cat,
That killed the Rat,
That ate the Malt,
That lay in the House that Jack built.